The Hero

Written by Tom Paxton   Illustrated by Don Vanderbeek

CelebrationPress

An Imprint of ScottForesman

On a hot and sunny day,
Engelbert came out to play.

All his friends, both large and small,
came with him to play some ball.

Engelbert yelled, "I smell smoke!"
His friends all thought it was a joke.

But from a house they heard a shout,
and Mrs. Mouse came running out.

5

Clouds of smoke were rising higher.
Mrs. Mouse cried, "Help! A fire!"

All the animals stopped their games
as they saw the orange flames.

7

Through the windows and the door,
smoke was blowing more and more.

8

The little house of white and brown
looked as if it might burn down.

Things looked bad for Mrs. Mouse.
She was going to lose her house!

"Help me save my house!" she cried.
"Carry all my things outside!"

11

Engelbert made no mistake.
He went running to the lake.

Filling up his trunk, he ran
back to where the fire began.

13

From his trunk he blew a spray,
and the fire was washed away.

The friends worked hard to make the house
clean and dry for Mrs. Mouse,

cheering as they marched away
for the hero of the day.
"HURRAY FOR ENGELBERT!"

16